WHY ARE YOU HERE?

VERY BRIEF FICTIONS
BY
SIMON COLLINGS

WHY ARE YOU HERE?

VERY BRIEF FICTIONS
BY
SIMON COLLINGS

ODD VOLUMES

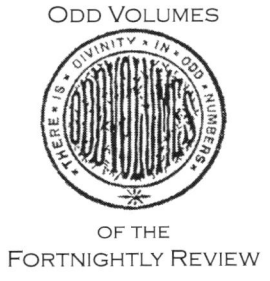

OF THE
FORTNIGHTLY REVIEW

LES BROUZILS
2020

Odd Volumes of

The Fortnightly Review

www.fortnightlyreview.co.uk

Editorial office:

Château Ligny
2 rue Georges Clemenceau
85260 Les Brouzils
France

ODD VOLUMES
2020

ISBN 978-0-9991365-6-0

Also by Simon Collings:

Out West, Albion Beatnik Press, 2017 (chapbook)
Stella Unframed, Red Ceilings, 2018 (chapbook)
Sanchez Ventura, Leafe Press, forthcoming 2021 (chapbook)

Contents

For Jane

Naturally things cannot in reality fit together the way the evidence does in my letter; life is more than a Chinese puzzle.

Franz Kafka (Letter to his father)

YOU HAD A SUITCASE

There seemed to be no one at the counter. The blind was drawn and behind the glass I could see a clutter of papers, a telephone. I remember you had a suitcase. You told me your name. What I don't remember is where you were going. Perhaps you never told me. The apartment I stayed in that night was filthy, no heating, the shower full of broken tiles. I don't remember a bed. Did I sleep? I tried to clean but had only a mop. I swept up the dirt as best I could, leaving it piled beside a vegetable patch at the end of the room. At dawn I returned to look for you. The station had been remodelled, but the information kiosk hadn't moved, and the blind was still down.

ᗷEETLES

The beetles infesting the bathroom were multiplying. They were small and black, not much bigger than a match head. Imogen had noticed a few of them soon after we arrived. While we were out getting something to eat more of them had appeared, and they were still on the increase. Neither of us could work out where they were coming from. The bathroom window was painted shut, so they weren't getting in from outside. 'I'm sure they're connected to that thing with the flashing green light in the hall,' Imogen said. 'We shouldn't have turned it off. It probably controls them somehow.' The purpose of the small electrical device, the size of a mobile phone, was a mystery. The folder of instructions which came with the flat made no mention of it, or of beetles. I searched the cupboards for insecticide without success, and it was too late now to go and buy any. The beetles sat on the walls and window frame, barely moving. They had become so numerous we decided to seal off the bathroom. I found a roll of duct tape in the utility room and we stuck it carefully round the edges of the door. It was close to midnight. 'I never thought it would be like this,' Imogen said, starting to cry. That was when I noticed the beetle on the wall above the bed.

SYNCHRONICITY

Dolores had been reading a story in the inflight magazine about strange coincidences – 'synchronicity' as the writer called it. One of these stories concerned a woman on a business trip who had reconnected with a childhood sweetheart after a chance encounter in a hotel bar, and later married him. Dolores suspected the story was a fabrication, it was just too improbable. But checking in at her hotel she found herself standing next to a man of around her own age who looked vaguely familiar. While the clerk verified her reservation the man turned towards her. 'Don't I know you?' he asked. 'Dolores Ramón,' she said holding out her hand. 'How extraordinary. I'm Martin, Martin Longmore.' 'This is so weird.' Dolores said, 'I was just reading about chance meetings like this on the plane.' They agreed to have dinner together, and Martin suggested a place nearby. 'I still can't believe it's happening,' Dolores said, when they'd taken their seats in the restaurant. 'Yes it's strange, but a very pleasant surprise.' 'Did you notice they gave us table 16? That's the age we were when we met.' 'I didn't see that,' Martin said. 'But now I think of it, I was in seat 16D on the plane.' The waiter brought menus and drew their attention to a large blackboard on the wall listing the evening's specials. Dolores looked over at the board, then froze. 'Oh my god,' she said. 'I don't believe it. My ex-husband is seated at the other end of the restaurant. He's with a woman.' Martin scanned the far end of the room. 'You mean over in the corner? But this is unbelievable, the woman he's with…is my ex-wife.'

⊘BJECT NO. 43

It hadn't moved since we first noticed it and I guessed it must be stuffed. Millions of them once roamed the plains but they were later hunted to near extinction. What this one was doing on our lawn was anyone's guess. Taking the shotgun I approached cautiously. It was an antique, as I'd thought. The hooves had small wheels attached and the parallel grooves in the turf showed where someone had trundled it over the grass. The left eye was missing, and here and there repairs had been made to tears in the hide, perhaps where moths had nibbled it. Underneath we discovered a flap exposing a chamber where a child or small adult might comfortably fit. Nickel-plated levers raised and lowered the head, opened the jaw.

ALLEZ, CALME

Our neighbour, P, grew up in Monaco where in his youth he was a member of a bodybuilding club. By taking up weights, he had hoped to overcome a childhood fear of being overpowered by strangers. He was also at this time a promising pianist, earning a living performing in cafés and nightclubs. One afternoon he was playing Satie, part of his usual repertoire, in a café where he appeared regularly. Part way through the *Gnossiennes*, a large bear of a man, unfamiliar to P, in an expensive but ill-fitting suit, took a seat in the window. When P reached the end of the final piece in the set, marked '*allez, calme*' in the score, one of the waiters came over to inform him that the gentleman by the window considered the music 'irritating' and would he play something more popular. P looked across at the gentleman, and began playing Satie's *Quatre Préludes*. After a few moments the offended customer rose from his seat and marched over to the piano. Precisely what happened next is the subject of legend, P being far too modest to give details. Suffice it to say, five minutes later his challenger was being escorted from the premises by three police officers, and P was seated again at the piano playing Satie. Stories circulated and P became something of a local celebrity. The episode later formed the basis for a popular Italian car commercial.

BURNING RING OF FIRE

There is nothing in the gallery, no paintings, no sculpture. People wander from one empty room to another, exchanging bemused expressions, imagining that perhaps it's a joke. The labels on the walls seem to be left over from a previous show, some partly peeled off, it's hard to tell. There's no information, no audio guide. 'Why did you come?' one label asks. 'What are you looking at?' asks another. 'Who are all these people?' A teenage girl, dressed as an Italian Renaissance Madonna and with a small naked child in her arms, periodically glides through the rooms. She makes eye contact with those she passes, holding their gaze for a moment with a look empty of expression. In the corner of the final room is an old jukebox, like a piece of abandoned scrap. Every ten minutes it lights up and plays a record – always the same record – Jonny Cash singing 'Burning ring of fire.'

ON THE TOURIST TRAIL

That evening, on her way home from work, Gloria found a party of Chinese tourists in the street outside her house. They were dressed in identical yellow fleeces bearing the name of a tour company, and taking turns to pose for selfies with her home in the background. 'What's going on?' she asked when she'd found the guide. 'Your house is famous,' the woman said. 'Everyone knows your house.' From what the young guide told her, Gloria understood that a novel about an accident-prone professor, by an obscure British writer from the 1950s, had recently been adapted for a Chinese mini-TV series. Now Gloria's house, the address at which the fictional professor was once supposed to have lived, was on the tourist trail. 'Many people will come,' the guide assured her. The next day Gloria found a young Chinese couple in her garden peering through the front window. They seemed put out when she asked them to leave. 'Isn't there a law against this?' she asked when she finally got through to someone at the local council. 'I'm afraid not,' said the official. 'Then what am I going to do?' 'Think of it as an opportunity,' the official said. 'Have you considered offering tours of the house, cream teas in the garden? It could be a goldmine. Of course you'll need a licence, but I don't see any problem.'

ROoM 33

It was years since I had last been in Paris, and I had no recollection of ever having stayed in the hotel where I was to spend the
next three nights. But the clerk at the reception desk greeted me
as though I were a regular. He seemed to know me though I was
almost certain I didn't know him. Could he be confusing me with
someone else? 'I've put you in the usual room,' he said, handing
me a key with the number 33 on it. 'I hope you'll find everything to
your satisfaction.' Confused by his assumption that I would know
the room he meant, I failed to ask directions and it took me a while
to locate it. I unlocked the door and found myself in an exact
replica of a room in a cheap hotel I had stayed in more than twenty
years before. I remembered quite clearly the faded rose-patterned
wallpaper, the ornate iron bedframe, the bolsters. It was a room
where I had spent three days with a woman I was having an affair
with, an affair which nearly destroyed my marriage. While I stood
there recalling that difficult period of my life the phone on the
bedside table started to ring. I picked up the heavy, black handset.
It was the receptionist calling. 'I forgot to mention that madame
rang earlier,' he said. 'She asked me to let you know that she will
be here in an hour.'

⊘BJECT NO. 135

It's unusual to find the leather case so well preserved. Apart from minor staining in the lower right-hand corner, this is one of the finest I have seen. Inside, the four balls nestle, each in its individual velvet-lined pocket, the original printed labels still intact. The white is marked M, the red F, the yellow Sol, the blue Mare. The red ball is of course at the top, the blue to the right and so on, each sphere marked with a delicate black line which divides the surface into hemispheres, each hemisphere inscribed with a line of indecipherable script written in an elaborate cursive hand. A slender, tapering baton fashioned from the wood of a yew, a silver ferule fitted to the narrower end, is secured in a shallow groove to the left of the four balls. Along the bottom of the case are the seven indentations where the missing charm figures should be.

⟅ILLEGIBLE

As soon as the coast was clear we began writing up our notes. In the pitch dark this was harder than I had expected, and in order not to overwrite what I had already jotted down I found I was having to leave a generous amount of space between lines, with the result that I was only able to get a few dozen words on each page. Despite my best efforts I was rapidly running out of paper. N had fared no better and was already on her last sheet. What were we to do? I decided to risk switching on a small torch which I had brought with me for just such an emergency, first wrapping it carefully in my handkerchief so as to diffuse the brightness. N looked nervous. 'What will HQ say?' she asked. I told her I had no intention of reporting this, and that if she didn't mention it no one would ever know. Could I trust her not to talk? She had always been a stickler for procedure, and I wasn't sure. Most of my notes, I could see, were incomprehensible. N's were equally illegible.

THE MEETING

My train had been delayed and I was ten minutes late arriving for the meeting, so when the taxi pulled up outside the hotel I jumped out, paid the driver, and rushed through the door. The hotel foyer was not what I had expected. The walls were dark red, and instead of the usual reception desk there was only a small table, placed just inside the door. Behind it sat a young woman who seemed to be wearing nothing but a negligée. In some confusion I asked if this was the hotel. She smiled, but said nothing. I started to feel flushed, and turned to leave, but found that the door through which I had entered was now a wall covered with the same red flock wallpaper as the rest of the room. I felt the surface for signs of a secret panel but the door seemed to have vanished. The woman behind the desk was observing my predicament with amusement. The only way out seemed to be through a curtained archway on the other side of the room, so I crossed the room and stepped through the gap in the drapes. I was on a narrow, brightly lit stage. The footlights dazzled me at first but I gradually became aware that I was facing a small auditorium filled with people who were watching expectantly. 'Does anyone know how to get to the hotel next door?' I asked. A few people tittered. 'Please,' I said, 'will someone help me?' This provoked a more sustained burst of laughter. Then a song began playing over the theatre's sound system, a Nina Simone number – 'Do I move you'. The woman from behind the desk had just slipped on to the stage behind me. She was wearing a long red evening gown, split to the thigh, a feather boa, and silver gloves. She glided across the stage towards me, and slowly began undoing my tie.

℘OINT OF VIEW

The other three had names, Xavier, Nisha, and Katherine, and brief descriptions of some of their physical characteristics were provided. For example Nisha's nervous laugh, the way her long black hair became unmanageable when she was caught in the rain. But they remained hazy, people I felt no great affection for, and perhaps was not meant to. My own identity was more seriously in doubt. Until then I had made little impression on the narrative, a kind of genial bystander no one recalled having missed. I could only hope that at some point someone might call my name. How did I know so much about these other people, about things which happened in private between them, events which I could not have known really took place, even had they told me about them? I was no more than a diffuse presence without definite character, a companion in all but name who saw everything and was nowhere. Having no specific role but to witness I felt neither envy nor delight at their varying fortunes, my shadow lingering in the background like Katherine's golden retrievers, and even they ignored me.

THE APARTMENT

On entering the apartment I was surprised to find that a number of the guests had arrived before me. They had evidently been there for some time, and were making themselves at home, lounging in armchairs or sitting on cushions on the floor. I had expected to be early, deliberately arriving in advance of the appointed time in order to enjoy a few private moments with our host, and to be in possession of the territory as it were when the others arrived. On my way there I had pictured the apartment, which I had not previously visited, visualising its pale blue striped wallpaper, the collection of antique carriage clocks, the paintings. I had seen photographs, and knew of his tastes from our frequent conversations, and the rooms were in many respects exactly as they had been described, though in other ways disconcertingly unfamiliar. G came over to greet me, and his manner was as open and genial as it had always been. I had thought of him as reclusive, a man who did not easily admit others into his company. But the presence of the other guests now left me unsure of my position and I found myself looking down at the carpet and noticing to my dismay that the lace of my right shoe had come untied.

THE CAFÉ

The owners of the café were a Japanese-American couple. The husband was into minimalism and the music of Morton Feldman was often playing quietly in the background. I had found it intriguing at first but the constant repetition of the note patterns began to wear on me after a while. I put up with it because I had a thing about the wife. 'It's because you're tense,' Aiko said. 'Take some deep breaths.' She placed my flat white on the table and adjusted her bra strap. 'Art teaches nothing about life,' she said. 'Just as life teaches us nothing about art.' The décor was spartan, wooden tables, white walls, no pictures. Her husband's only extravagance was an antique shogi set dating from around 1900. He kept it behind the counter in case a customer came in one day who knew how to play. I was thinking of learning the game, so I'd have an excuse to spend more time there.

VERNE'S NEMESIS

Reading *Twenty Thousand Leagues under the Sea* it's hard not to be struck by the fervour of Captain Nemo's revolutionary idealism. His open-handed support for liberation movements around the world, financed with gold bullion recovered from the sunken wrecks of Spanish galleons, is unswerving. But Verne gives only one identifiable example of a struggle supported by Nemo, that of the Cretan Revolt against Ottoman rule in the 1860s. This uprising attracted considerable public support in Europe and North America, and the Greek rebels could have been financed by any number of liberal philanthropists. It did not require someone with Nemo's beliefs to step in to support the revolutionaries, and we can only speculate about the other groups fighting tyranny and oppression which benefitted from the largesse of the inventor of the *Nautilus*. Verne, in the person of the bourgeois Professor Aronnax, eventually jumps ship, literally and metaphorically distancing himself from Nemo, a character seemingly too radical to be comfortably embraced any longer within the pages of the novel. Nemo had, after all, sunk a US naval vessel, with the loss of its entire crew. But Verne does not do away with Nemo. Whether the *Nautilus* survives the whirlpool at the end of the narrative is left open, the militant Nemo surreptitiously slipping away perhaps to continue the struggle, a surrogate for suppressed desires his author dared not acknowledge, even to himself. Four years later, in *The Mysterious Island*, we encounter Nemo again, strangely aged and failing in health, and with the dates of his exploits hopelessly at variance with the earlier book, as though Verne wants to underline the fact that this is all invention, a work of fiction. This time

Nemo is put to rest, his corpse entombed forever in the scuppered *Nautilus*.

ℰPISODE 13

Frank had been talking non-stop all morning and Bill was beginning to lose patience. Either they got to switch roles in the next episode or he wouldn't be answerable for his actions. The script writers were taking this too far. He thought about throttling Frank, wringing the life out of him with his bare hands. But he knew that wasn't going to happen. They had plans for Frank and a trip into the hereafter wasn't part of the plot. Bill knew he was fated to always end up cast as the strong, silent type, the good listener. But why? Didn't he have things to contribute? He was sure he had something to say, ideas of his own, but what were they? A hand was waving in front of his face. 'Are you listening to me?' Frank asked.

STORM

J was in the car park below. I could see him clearly, his broad familiar frame braced against the driving rain. He had once been a popular figure, and I was something of a follower myself. The fatalism of his sombre poetry appealed to me in my youth, with its bleak indifferent landscapes, the relentless cycle of death. But his star had waned, his later poems deteriorating into something of a parody of his earlier work, and few people now appeared to read him. Out there in the night he looked a diminished figure. Arms spread wide, he seemed to be wrestling the wind, as though the storm were the monstrous script of a universal drama in which he was doomed to play a part. Yellow birch leaves streamed down around him, covering the wet tarmac. It was a titanic struggle, into which he threw everything he had. Finally, after an intense and lengthy tussle the wind got the better of him, lifting him off the ground and carrying him away over the slate-black roofs of the houses.

ORANG-UTAN

The chicken only takes twenty minutes to cook, so there is nothing much to do until their guests arrive. Sharon and Barry go through to the front room with their drinks and switch on the TV. Sharon surfs channels until she finds a holiday programme about Turkey. They watch middle-aged couples in swimsuits wading in the sea, then a tour group visiting the ruins of an ancient Greek temple. The prices of apartments and hotel rooms scroll across the screen while the presenter enthuses about the country over a background of Turkish folk music. 'Didn't they have a bombing there?' Sharon says. 'Or was that somewhere else?' She flicks through more channels, stopping at a documentary about orang-utans which the programme's narrator says are threatened with extinction. There's a group of wildlife people trying to save them from the effects of logging in the forest where they live. On the screen a family of orang-utans sit munching leaves, like they know something's happening but they aren't sure what. 'Watching them eat is making me feel hungry,' Sharon says and goes into the kitchen. She comes back with a plate of salami in one hand and a bowl of olives in the other. She puts the plates on the floor and snacks while they watch more of the documentary. Barry tries to imagine the orang-utans looking out through the TV, watching him and Sharon sprawled on the sofa, as if they're on the set of a reality TV show. He wonders what they're thinking.

⑨ON'T GIVE UP

'Don't give up!' the flyer said. Just those three words, in large, bold print, plus a phone number. She found it in the basket of her bicycle when she left work. It was printed on pale pink paper. Give up what, she wondered. She hadn't been planning on giving anything up. She looked around at the other bikes but could see no more leaflets scattered about. Could someone have left it specifically for her? Her bike was in the middle of two rows of cycle racks, and it seemed unlikely the leaflet could have been discarded there. Maybe it had been dropped by the wind. It felt like a trap, some sort of advertising gimmick. Taking out her phone she dialled the number, thinking she'd give someone a piece of her mind. 'Thank you for calling,' a computerised voice said. 'All our operators are busy right now, but we value your call and someone will be with you as soon as possible. Please, don't give up.' This was followed by twenty seconds of muzak, then the same message was repeated. She was starting to get annoyed. How long did they expect her to hang on? She listened to the message several times more. Maybe it was some sort of endurance test. She looked at the leaflet again, wondering what she should do. 'Don't give up,' the automated voice said.

THE EVIDENCE

That's you, they tell me. Remember that happening? The locations I seem to recognise, but I don't believe the person I am watching in the video is me. The filming was mostly done at night, and always from a distance. The blurry figure on the screen could be an actor, someone of my approximate build who had studied my habits, the way I walk, the way I hold myself. There are no close ups. The images seem to relate to something from a long time ago. They play the video again. I don't remember any of the events shown. Only the locations appear familiar. Try to remember, they say. I watch the footage over again. Filming in the streets I often frequented, the lobbies of office buildings, a railway station from which I travelled on occasion, would have been easily arranged. But why would anyone do that? This could simply be a case of mistaken identity. The evidence is circumstantial. Something about the figure on the screen doesn't ring true. Is this a dramatisation, a fiction? Try to remember they say, it's important you try to remember.

ℕATURAL REMEDY

'Rosemary oil is anti-viral,' the shop assistant tells N. 'A lot of people don't know that.' She's wearing a surgical facemask and rubber gloves. A number of small bottles are lined up on the counter in front of her. 'Turmeric milk is also good,' she volunteers. 'It generates red blood cells, besides piling your body with essential nutrients and acting as a health tonic.' N hasn't seen her in the shop before. She's attractive, he thinks, even in the mask. Under different circumstances he might have suggested meeting up, but just now that's obviously inappropriate. He adjusts his own facemask. 'Give me a bottle of the rosemary oil,' he says. 'I ought to try this.' The lockdown could go on for weeks, even months. He wonders how long he'll have to sustain his new-found interest in alternative medicine.

MARIGOLDS

The narrow room was hot and crowded with people. A young man in a suit handed me a chit of paper which I attempted to read. It seemed to be a set of instructions but the words kept dissolving before I could make them out. The man looked at me blankly, then signalled for me to move on. There was a door to the left through which I hoped I might escape the press of bodies. But this led only to a low-ceilinged gallery, where I was forced to walk hunched over, picking my way awkwardly through the slumbering bodies of the inhabitants. A narrow archway at the far end opened onto an even more constricted space, shrouded in shadow. The floor was covered with earth and had been planted with marigolds. The only way out appeared to be through a hatchway, about the width of my body, low down in the wall opposite. Around me in the spectral gloom the orange blooms glowed with hypnotic intensity.

THE LIBRARY

Among D's many and varied works was a treatise entitled *Principles of non-linear classification* – an early monograph advocating the abandonment of the Dewey decimal system in favour of allowing books to be shelved according to the subjective associations between texts. Thus Lautréamont's *Maldoror* might be filed next to a pamphlet containing photographs of murmurations of starlings, while Schopenhauer's *Die Welt als Wille und Vorstellung*, could be placed adjacent to a book about poodles. 'All development of thought arises out of transgression,' he wrote.

D's marginalia helped establish the associations, which were of course multiple, and changed over time. He was constantly re-organising his voluminous library, and this was part of his principle. Books he had read in his youth, and not understood, became later in his life much-loved companions, and were moved from the margins to the centre of his collection. Scholars of D's work have spent many hours trying to reconstruct the life of particular volumes, and the works with which they were 'associated', in their efforts to elucidate some of the more obscure passages in D's writings.

D argued that 'subjective classification' created an organic system which opened possibilities for new discoveries, by constantly eroding boundaries and reshaping categories of thought. *Principles of non-linear classification* gives the example of a man who finds a pebble on a beach that strikes him as exceptionally beautiful, 'begging to be picked up'. Later he realises that the shingle contains a bewildering number of similarly fine pebbles. In an attempt to console him, his wife takes the pale-pink oval stone and places it on the windowsill next to an oddly shaped piece of driftwood and the skull of a crow. The stone seems to belong there and the man realises that it is the juxtaposition of these objects which is the source of their vitality, not the objects themselves. Significance is created by the relationship between the objects. 'Stripped of the burden of meaning, the pink stone discovered its potentiality when placed on the sill by his wife.'

The making of a library was for D a work of time. The fact that as he grew older the content of innumerable volumes in his collection was largely forgotten did not matter. The library became a metaphor for memory, and in particular his own failing powers of recall, which he believed were mirrored in the society around him. As he says in *The Question for Philosophy:* 'Our inability to recognise once familiar landmarks plunges us into confusion.' But this for D was a generative process, destruction leading to new possibilities, opportunity being created out of ruin. The library was there, unlike the past, always available to be rediscovered, reinventing itself continually in the light of fresh associations.

DESTINY

There's an inevitability which the viewer can never anticipate, even with hindsight, about the scene with the dead blackbird. She's holding a bouquet of fading tulips, open to being persuaded, but still shaken by the incident. The brilliant yellow of the blackbird's beak echoes the colour of the flowers. Now that the urgency has dissipated she is isolated, adrift in the dusty light of a series of lame excuses she can't excuse. A woman's voice tells us this. Spring has arrived late and the intricate steps involved in its hesitations have been a constant distraction. Could this be her destiny, she wonders out loud. Waiting for the right moment to introduce itself?

QUESTION 7

Given this situation does A: (i) write a long, rambling and incoherent email to his artist friend C recalling episodes from the years they studied together, a time when A still entertained hopes of becoming someone famous; (ii) have a conversation with his dog F about the inexplicable success of B whose work he has never rated, and possibly also D who he has not previously considered as part of this equation; (vi) feed the dog toast while listening to a vinyl recording of Zemlinsky's second string quartet which he bought as a schoolboy, the record turning out to have a nasty scratch towards the end of the third movement which he doesn't remember being there before; (xxii) receive an unexpected visit from the author of this poem who insists his self-indulgence has to stop, resulting in a scuffle which the dog thinks is a game and tries to join in, an altercation which only ends when C unexpectedly turns up on the doorstep; (xxxi) wake up on the sofa with a bad headache having just been dreaming that the sound of the dog pawing at the door to be let out was D methodically destroying his record and CD collection; (xliv) tie up the author in order to wrest control of his, A's, destiny but then not know what to do with this new-found freedom; (li) wonder how, with the author now securely bound and gagged, this is all going to end.

EPISODE 17

'I want a speaking part,' Bill said. 'I'm sick of just being an extra.' Frank looked taken aback. This wasn't like Bill. 'What sort of thing did you have in mind?' he asked. 'Our distance from the divine is both infinite and proximate,' Bill said. Frank pondered, then cracked his knuckles. 'Are you feeling OK? You don't seem yourself.' 'Who am I?' Bill asked. 'That's what I want to know. Who am I?' 'Take it easy buddy,' Frank said. 'Maybe you should start with something a little simpler, like 'Hi, I'm Bill' or 'that's *really* funny'.' 'I've signed up for a course of elocution lessons,' Bill said. Frank groaned. 'Are these glasses half empty, or half full?' 'I have ambition, Frank. I want to be someone,' Bill insisted. 'You don't know this, but I once played a severed head in a film about the French Revolution. I really think I could go places.'

Ⓕ FAMILY HISTORY

After my mother died, my father developed an interest in family history. Tracking down names, births, marriages, was fairly straightforward, but who any of these people were had slid ineluctably into the shadows of history. I began inventing stories about some of these distant forebears, including one about a boy called George, my great, great, great, great, great grandfather in fact, who grew up in the parish of Selbourne. I told my father how George had once sewn the head and wings of a falcon onto the body of a grass snake, and then had presented this magical creature to the Rev Gilbert White, earning for his pains a clip round the ear. My father scoffed at this tale. Months later I came across a collection of White's scientific writings at a charity book sale. Idly flicking through its pages, I read this: "April 25. Village lad brought me a 'griffon' this morning, head and wings of a falcon stitched crudely to the tail end of a snake. Sent him off with a stern admonishment."

THE CRUMB

Yuki sat cross-legged on the bench while they ate lunch. Eric didn't know her well but he listened with interest as she spoke of the clocks of nineteenth-century Japan, which apparently did not keep time, and were not meant to. Then she started telling him about the Bells of Time. She had ordered toast spread with guacamole and offered him one of the slices, which she said she couldn't eat. While he was biting into the bread a small crumb flew out of his mouth and landed in her glass of water. He felt embarrassed, but she seemed not to have noticed. By this time she had moved on to string theory, and the fact that a surprising number of string theorists are Japanese. No opportunity presented itself for Eric to draw attention to the crumb. The Buddhist traditions of her country, she was explaining, meant string theory came more easily to Japanese people. It had something to do with their concept of time. Eric was finding it hard to focus on anything other than the small particle of toasted ciabatta resting on the meniscus of water in front of him.

THE PUBLISHER

Sales of my second novel were not going well, largely, I suggest, because of the incompetence of my publisher. Passing along the street near his office I found him lying in the gutter, intoxicated, his trousers and pants pulled down around his knees. His pubic hair had the same gingery-red colour as his beard. He was conscious and was railing loudly against someone or something, and he eyed me savagely. I didn't wait to find out what had upset him. Possibly it had something to do with my book. When I reached home I put on a DVD of tropical fish, to try to calm my nerves. The under-water sounds and the varied shapes and colours of the fish soon took effect, and after a couple of hours I was able to return, with something like my customary vigour, to the story I had begun writing earlier that morning.

ACROSS THE VALLEY

The long opening shot is of a painting. A woman stands on a patio, looking across a garden at the lights in the valley below, lights just visible through the mist. She has her back towards us, her shoulders covered by a pale green shawl, inviting us into the illusory space of the picture, urging us to see what she sees. The scene has been painted in photographic detail. The frame widens, the camera panning to the right. The painting, we discover, hangs opposite a pair of French windows which open onto a patio, from where, through the skeins of mist, lights are visible in the valley below. A breeze blows in at the window, bringing with it the hum of distant traffic. Through the French windows we can see a woman standing in the garden, draped in a lime green shawl, her back towards us. 'Where are you?' a voice says, a woman's voice. (The actor who plays the woman also lives in a house overlooking a valley, where later we glimpse her face for the first time reflected in a mirror.) The camera advances toward the open French windows. The woman seems unaware of the camera's presence, of the voice. The valley below is shrouded in mist.

THEORY

And it is certainly arguable that, at some deep level, Wordsworth saw in the person of the blind beggar the incarnation of the unseeing Milton, the brief text hanging upon his form a token for the poet's works, works which Wordsworth himself wished to supplant. This sudden revelation, however obscurely apprehended, of not just the physical blindness but also the intellectual blindness of the 17th century poet, is experienced by Wordsworth both as an 'admonishment' in relation to his ambitions in the literary sphere, and as a spur to his aspiration toward greatness – not for its own sake but for the betterment of Man. Indeed, one might even suggest that here is another of those instances of Oedipal rage which Jerome Freidhof argues so persuasively Wordsworth displays toward Milton in several other passage in *The Prelude*.* Or one might argue, following Debord, that Wordsworth here effects a subtly disguised *détournement* with the object of exposing, even if only subliminally, the hollowness of vision underlying Milton's achievement. If readers find this fanciful let them ask themselves why it is a *man with impaired vision* who strikes Wordsworth amongst the throng, rather than a woman with a cleft palate, or a legless child.

*Freidhof, J., 'Wordsworth's Oedipus complex', *Journal of Abstruse Literary Theories*, vol 6, issue 4, Nov/Dec 1986.

LAST WORDS

One of the conditions in my uncle's will was that we publish in the national press full-page advertisements containing what he called his 'last words'. He was a private man, hard to engage in general conversation, though he had held several important positions in government and industry. He gave no intimation to any of us of the sentiments expressed in this final statement, and it came as a surprise to many. It read: 'There are a number of people who caused me considerable pain and misery during my life. They know who they are, and their families know who they are, so I have no need to name them. Some of these people acted out of deliberate malice, others from weakness. Being told this was "only human" afforded me no consolation. There can be no excuse. Their conduct was vile and contemptible. I do not believe in God, and do not look to some future life for justice. I am in my grave. But I want them to know I never forgave them for what they did to me.'

☉BJECT NO. 14

In the gathering dusk the neighbourhood looked unfamiliar, but I knew the car was around here somewhere. All I had to do was walk up and down the rows of parked cars until I spotted its familiar shape. The streets were virtually empty of people, but anyway what would I have said had anyone passed me? I could hardly ask if they had seen a silver Passat. Then turning a corner I ran into what I took to be a small dog, a toy poodle to be precise, though its hair was bright pink. 'Can I help you?' it asked in a husky American accent. 'A robot,' I thought. 'That's right,' it said, wagging its tail. It eyed me quizzically, its head cocked on one side. Clearly I was going to have to be careful here. I tried to empty my mind of thoughts, and set off down the street, the robot dog following. 'Hey sarge, I don't think you told me your name,' it said. 'Looking for your car, by any chance?' I pressed on along the street, trying to shake it off. 'Some sort of neighbourhood watch scheme,' I thought. 'Not even warm,' the robot poodle said.

THE DOUBLE

I first noticed him in a café, where my wife and I had just been having lunch. He was reading a newspaper, his face partly concealed, but there was something about his posture, and the way he moved, which reminded me of myself. Later that day I saw him again when I went out to post a letter. He was seated behind the wheel of a car parked just down the street. Our eyes met as I passed and the likeness of his face to mine was unmistakeable. I told Carol about him, but she thought I must be imagining things. A few days later we went to the cinema, and there he was again, seated a few rows behind us. 'My doppelganger's here,' I whispered, 'behind you and to the left.' Carol turned around and surveyed the rows of seats. 'Where?' she said, turning back. 'I can't see anyone who looks like you.' Then the film began, preventing further discussion, and by the time it ended the man had gone. Later that evening I found him in the kitchen, laughing with Carol. They were drinking, and he was wearing one of my shirts. Carol looked startled. 'Who are you? How did you get in?' she asked nervously. 'It's me, Philip.' I said, but she showed no sign of recognition. The man got up from the table where they had been sitting. 'I think you'd better leave,' he said. 'But I live here,' I protested. 'Get him out of here Philip,' Carol said, addressing not me but my lookalike. 'Please, get him out of here.' He was surprisingly strong, and despite my protests I found myself being bundled irresistibly towards the door. As we passed the hall mirror I caught a glimpse of my face. It was that of a total stranger.

cANOTHER LIFE (1)

Half-way round the exhibition I found I was in need of the bathroom. An attendant pointed me down a long gallery, to a door at the end, and I left my wife in front of a video installation called 'Another life' to go in search of relief. The door from the gallery led on to a stairwell with a sign for 'toilets' pointing downwards. I descended several flights but found no trace of the promised facilities. Finally, at the bottom of the stairs was a door marked 'Gents'. I pushed on this and entered a small ante-room with hand basins where I found an attendant, a young man of African heritage. He looked at me without expression and motioned toward a bead curtain at the end of the room which gave access to a kind of outhouse made of sticks and dried palm fronds. I wondered if this was some sort of eco-experiment, or perhaps part of the exhibition. A hole had been dug in the middle with a plank across it, and it was with much relief that I urinated into the latrine. I went back through the curtain to wash my hands, but emerged to my surprise, not into the room with the washbasins, but on to a narrow path of red earth leading to a cluster of mud-brick houses with corrugated-iron roofs. From the shade of the houses a dozen or so villagers were watching me guardedly.

SEEING THINGS

'Such places harbour unusual energies,' Saffron is saying, 'spiritual presences you might call them. They appear to people in visions or waking dreams, sometimes as human or animal figures. It's the land itself that conserves these energies.' This is the first time Jo has met Saffron and she is wondering why Luis introduced them as 'fellow poets'. She glances around at the other party guests, looking for someone she might draw into their conversation. But everyone seems absorbed in animated discussion. Luis, their host, is busy with the barbeque. He looks up for a moment and waves at her. Jo waves back. 'Of course it isn't everyone who can tune into these energies,' Saffron says. 'Only people with the necessary sensitivity are going to experience those visions.' Jo finds herself stifling a yawn, but Saffron seems not to notice. She's talking about an archaeological site she visited in Turkey where she saw the shadows of figures moving about in the ruins, the trace presence of people who had lived there thousands of years before. Jo nods. Her glass is empty, and has been for a while. 'I think I might go and...' she says, but Saffron carries on talking. 'You think I'm crazy, don't you?' she says. Jo answers 'no', that she's been following with interest. 'Well let me see,' Saffron continues. She pauses for a moment as though searching her memory for something. 'You're working on a sequence of poems just now, about moon goddesses, is that right?' 'How on earth did you know that?' Jo asks. 'I haven't told a soul about them.' 'I can't explain how I see these things,' Saffron says. 'They just come to me. I suppose it's some sort of gift.'

LA VIDA ES UN CARNIVAL

Somewhere on the other side a woman was singing in spite of the regulations. The words 'braced' and 'translucent' may have been used though it isn't certain. We talked about people with a family resemblance, afraid they might arrive at any moment. Eventually a small group of us decided to go down there. In the main square, papier-mâché maquettes had been hoisted into the trees; each wearing the colours of sunrise, the beach doubling as reminiscence. Transferred into another language the phrasing became a reef. A breeze came in off the sea, the scent familiar though hard to place, hints of cinnamon, wild oranges. The yacht too was memory.

The Hotel

Coming to and finding myself without a stitch on I decided I would try to get back to my hotel, which I estimated was about ten minutes away. Fortunately the avenue was crowded with people, and by losing myself in the throng I was more or less able to conceal my nakedness. Pressed close as I was against the pedestrians around me, it was hard for anyone to notice the full extent of my predicament. There was a marked chill in the early evening air, and the warmth of the bodies surrounding me happily afforded some protection against the cold. But the crowd moved slowly, so slowly that at times we appeared to be making little progress. I had no choice but to follow the general advance as I didn't want to draw attention to myself by trying to force a way through. I could see up ahead a neon sign with the name of my hotel on it, though I didn't remember the hotel being on this street. Perhaps there were two hotels with the same name, I thought. I was sure mine had been on a side street. I had no means of checking of course, and in fact I was no longer sure what the name of my hotel was.

Missing

When we got to the viewing place it was much busier than we'd expected. There's a sign there, 'Sublime View', and next to it the place you're supposed to stand for the perfect shot. Know where I mean? The spot where they painted the pair of feet? People were hanging around, jostling to have their turn, and William just kind of snapped. 'Let's get in the car,' he said, so we did. His face was set like…I don't know how to describe it. Like he was grieving. We drove down the hill and at the bottom he suddenly turned off onto this track heading out into the desert. He didn't say anything, just kept driving until we hit the gully and the car wouldn't go any further. Then he got out and started walking off into the bush. That was about three hours ago.

OBJECT NO. 54

To the tongue the taste is bitter, metallic. It's waxy to the touch, feels almost perfectly spherical, and given its size is surprisingly dense. A small indentation at one point on its surface is perhaps a trace left by the process of its making, or the place where a stalk was attached. Dropped on the floor it makes a dull thud and rolls away, and I have some difficulty locating it again. I may have lost consciousness, or perhaps I slept for a while. As I crawl about the floor I wonder if the object could have been taken away while I slumbered, or if perhaps I dreamed it. Traces of its odour seemingly remain on my fingers. Eventually I find it some distance away, if it is the same one, of which I cannot be certain, though it's of a similar size and weight, a single indentation in its surface as before.

ᎠÉCOR

Nadia had taken the job as a chambermaid at a big city hotel to earn the money she needed to support her painting. The hotel was part of an international chain, the company priding itself on its sense of style. Every guest-room was hung with an artwork, each canvas a variant on a general theme of abstract shapes and bright colours. Nadia hardly noticed them at first, intent on making up the rooms for new occupants. But after a while the insipid designs began to irritate her. She started to make her own additions, discreetly at first, so that no one would notice, a few words stencilled at an angle across an area of the picture where they blended with the general lines of the composition: 'two of a kind', 'trash', 'goes with the décor'. No one seemed to detect what she was doing. As time passed she became bolder. 'This is utter shit' she stencilled on one picture in large letters, and on another: 'puke.' Guests began remarking on the hotel's distinctive artistic policy, and comments appeared online, many extolling the artworks in the rooms. The hotel management was mystified. When a well-known dealer began asking about the painter, they realised the collection had commercial value. But who, they wondered, was the artist?

The Rue Morgue Murders

Holmes had a number of scientific journals spread out around him, and several travel books about Borneo. There was a gleam in his eye which suggested he had made a startling discovery. 'You'll remember, Watson, that Dupin concluded that the murders in the Rue Morgue were perpetrated by an escaped orang-utan belonging to a sailor lately arrived from Indonesia. Dupin was, I'm afraid, in spite of his undoubted analytical abilities, ill-informed about the behaviour of primates. The orang-utan is, by all accounts, an extremely gentle beast, and roused to displays of aggression only when physically threatened. There are no known cases of the creatures attacking humans. So it is hard to believe that an orang-utan entering the room of the two women would have felt sufficiently endangered that it was motivated to kill them, let alone stuff one of them up the chimney. There's only one species capable of this type of senseless violence, and that is *Homo sapiens*. The murders in my view must have been the work of the sailor, a man of psychopathic tendencies I suspect, and a skilful dissembler, who was capable of taking in Dupin and as a result escaped justice. One can only guess what further atrocities the man went on to commit.'

Going Up

Out on the balcony A's drag artist friend is talking about 'replenishing minerals'. It was in the news apparently, a slow downbeat of an idea gumming up the waste disposal. Our host appears discouraged by the indeterminacy of the project. The structure is now on jacks and due to be lifted higher. No one knows where else to go with it. Noises from the street, suggest a procession, or gridlocked traffic, an emergency vehicle trying to find a way through. Meanwhile the party '...meanders into a fluid execution of many details.' H advocates more granular approaches, a way of bringing everything down to eye level, the logic crepuscular though referencing an earlier system of flags. T suggests a classical analogy involving masks. Later the meaning wanders off on its own past the familiar landmarks though there's still no sign of a border.

The Paths

I look up and catch a glimpse of the path along which I've come, or I picture myself doing so, the traces already laid long since, awaiting my arrival, or if not *my* arrival that of someone like me who might act as the agent for whatever was meant to happen, a role fulfilled on this occasion by me, as events turned out. Let's say it was a result of circumstance, the product of a particular conjunction of factors, both internal and external, if such a distinction can be made, a moment in the turbulent buffeting of experience when the confluence of forces points in one direction and the flow carries us like a swimmer lacking the strength to breast the current. But this implies a struggle and there was none. How or when that moment arrived is difficult to say, whether I willed it, however unintentionally, or was taken unawares, caught off balance as it were and provoked into action where in other circumstances I might have proceeded differently. That moment can never now be reconstructed with any certitude, the impression already a blur, the sequence of events becoming confused, so that in the telling of it I find I have invented a version which now obscures other possibilities, omitting important details, a rationalisation after the fact hiding an obvious motive I can't or won't acknowledge, and of which I remain completely unaware. Yet I remember moving, and considering for a fleeting moment whether this was the right thing to be doing, a passing instant in which I might have opted for a different course but did not for reasons I can no longer articulate, and perhaps never actually debated with myself, those other options simply appearing like paths into a wood glimpsed from the window of a moving car which someone else was driving.

ꓶAUNE

In 1959 the avant-garde composer K read in an antique musi-cological dictionary an account of an unusual instrument. The entry described: 'an oblong cabinet made of rosewood, inlaid with mother of pearl, its interior fitted with resonating chambers through which the sound is magnified to a pleasing volume, the working parts being concealed within.' A small brass handle on one side of the box was turned to produce the tune, which varied according to the mood of the player. Distantly related to both the hurdy-gurdy and the harmonium, of which it was a kind of cross-bred offspring, the device achieved a level of subtlety suited to the ears of refined listeners. The person selected to turn the machinery was chosen by lot from among the assembled audience, so that no one knew whether the music would be merry or melancholy, dance like or a dirge. On one infamous occasion a young woman in the eighth month of pregnancy was the person upon whom the choice fell. The sounds she produced were so visceral and sugges-tive that the court Kapellmeister had to bring the performance to a premature close. On another occasion an elderly man, a widower, conjured from the ornate cabinet sounds so ethereal the assembled courtiers thought they were hearing angels. In later years, a specific post of 'master of the duke's music cabinet' was created so that one person and one only performed on the apparatus, producing an elegant and measured sound in keeping with the tastes of the period. In the late eighteenth century, the rapid advances of musical technology rendered the device quaint and anachronistic, and it fell into disuse. Intrigued, K made enquiries and discovered the instrument still existed. After lengthy negotiations the family who owned it agreed to allow him to include the music box in a piece for chamber ensemble, which the composer titled *Laune*. At the premier K himself turned the handle of the ancient cabinet, the first person to have done so in 170 years. The sound produced was a complete surprise, an intermittent drone pitched somewhere between G# and A, strangely apt as an accompaniment to the other players' parts, and imbuing the whole piece with a deep sense of nostalgia. When asked about his mood during the performance K said he had no memory of the event.

The Composer

I had just read in the newspaper of a female composer I hadn't heard of before, and thought of writing to V who I knew would be interested. A little research online turned up a number of recordings of the composer's works. One of these I noticed had been listened to 12,739 times, and several people had posted comments. I was surprised, considering the slight attention contemporary composers of serious music usually attract, and also somewhat disappointed. The composer was obviously better known than I had realised, and I started to feel my 'discovery' of her had unmasked the superficiality of my knowledge of the world of contemporary music. My claim to know anything about the subject, in fact, had been exposed. How had I persuaded myself I had something novel to share with V, who was far more knowledgeable than me on this subject? I decided I would not write to V in the way I had proposed, full of spontaneous enthusiasm, as this would almost certainly lay me open to further humiliation.

LANDSLIDE

The morning after the landslip the usual crowd of fortune seekers arrived. We watched them through the antique naval binoculars Dan gave us, sitting out on the sundeck. They were erecting some sort of apparatus on the beach, a high pitched whine generated by the electrical equipment driving the seabirds frantic. It had rained steadily for weeks and there was nothing unusual about the cliff face sliding into the sea. We'd seen it enough times to make it a foregone conclusion. Dan said he could imagine it blindfold. They all had hip flasks and drank steadily while they worked over the spoil in a flanking manoeuvre. The one Dan calls 'the colonel' was in it up to his knees, wrestling with the tangles of rusty wire. His t-shirt said: Mix & Match, a sort of personal motto, or maybe a slogan advertising something. Of course they won't find anything, they never do, though they keep coming back. Dan thinks it will all blow over when the rouble strengthens.

ᴄAZUCAR NEGRA

The harbour too was beyond recall. It was the winter solstice, the tide a long way out, and the air redolent of citrus and crushed cane. Expressed as an equation it might have been a new opening. In the car park life-size models of angels with brass trumpets hung suspended on wires, their wings glowing in the fading light. I chose to leave the others and go down there. The people on the quayside were strangers, and I spoke with each of them in turn. The words 'braced' and 'translucent' may have been used though it isn't certain. From a boat out at sea we could hear the sound of a woman singing, her elaborate coloratura lost in the wind.

ℰPISODE 20

Bill hadn't had an original thought in a long time. In fact it had been so long he couldn't think back to when exactly it was, let alone recall what the thought had been. The more he considered, the more he wondered if he had ever, strictly speaking, had a genuinely novel idea. Back in the distant past he thought he had once had ideas of his own, that at least was the image that took shape in his mind. But he was hard pressed to think of particular examples, and when he did finally recall something it was an idea he remembered he had subsequently discovered was something others had already thought of, in some instances many years before. This was something he recollected happening on a number of occasions. He had the feeling not of being a source of autonomous, free thoughts, but of ideas entering his mind from outside, the concepts arising not from any effort on his part, but coalescing out of the swirl of language in his head, like shadowy figures emerging from the mist.

BIRDSONG

It was only four o'clock but dusk was already falling when we turned into our road. As we neared the house my husband pointed out the sound of birdsong coming from a tall *Leylandii* in a neighbour's garden. The couple there had only recently moved in and we were yet to meet them. There seemed to be a whole flock of birds in their tree, warbling and chittering as though it were the first day of spring. We decided to get closer to see what kind of birds could be making so much noise at this time of year – some unusual winter visitor perhaps, driven south by the cold weather. The singing of the birds had lifted our mood, and had filled us both with a sense of unexpected excitement. As we crept up to the tree the chattering continued, but we could see no actual birds, though the branches were shaking as if from movement within. Perplexed, my husband stepped on to the neighbour's lawn and peered cautiously in among the foliage. After a few moments he beckoned me to approach and I too peered into the branches. I could see small cylinders taped to some of the branches, connected by wires, which were vibrating. And attached to the trunk were two small speakers from which the trilling of the birds poured forth into the gathering gloom.

OTHER LIVES (2)

After parking the land cruiser Nene took the stairs from the under-ground car park to the office. He'd just returned to Nairobi from up country, a four hour drive. The stairwell looked unfamiliar, and at first he thought it must have been redecorated, but as he climbed he realised he was in a building he did not recognise. He could hear voices coming from above and he climbed higher. It sounded like a party. On the second-floor landing he pushed open a door and stepped into a large ballroom full of white people in expensive clothes, drinking and talking. Along one side of the room was a table laden with food, and at the far end a large banner said: '2020 Artfest: Other Worlds, Other Lives'. A woman in a blue cocktail dress detached herself from the crowd of guests and came over to him. 'You must be one of the performers,' she said. 'Let's find you something to eat.'

The Lake

The people in the next room were quietly discussing my fate. The door was ajar and I could hear the murmur of their conversation, though only the occasional word was intelligible. After a while they got up and left, locking the outside door behind them. I heard an elevator, then silence. I had only one means of escape, through a grimy skylight in the ceiling of the room they had just vacated, and which I now entered. I was soon on the roof. At the end of the building I found a fire escape, and at the bottom I emerged onto a wide tiled patio overlooking the lake. An elderly woman stood a few yards away, near a bed of flowering shrubs. She was gazing out over the water, wrapped in a towel, her hair covered by a bathing cap. Was she associated with my captors, or just an ordinary hotel guest? She looked up as I approached and smiled. The air had seemed unusually still when I was climbing down from the roof, but a sudden gust of wind now caused her towel to flap open, revealing that she was naked, and exposing her pubic hair. She seemed unconcerned, perhaps even amused by this. 'Fancy a dip?' she asked.

HERMIT WANTED

Here we are, 'Hermit Wanted'. 'Lower Loxley Hall seeks to engage a person of suitable character and demeanour to occupy the hermitage, originally built in 1760, situated within the great park. The hermitage consists of a small grotto, constructed from rocks, which has recently been refurbished to comply with health and safety standards.' Sounds comfy. 'The post-holder will occupy the grotto when the house and grounds are open to the public. The successful candidate will be required to grow their hair and beard,' – you already qualify on that one – 'and to don eighteenth century costume, which will be supplied. Suitable reading matter, food, and fresh water will also be provided.' Sounds perfect. You can sit there reading all day, lunch is free, and you'll save on your heating bills.

CHIMERA

If this were a dream, a typical interpretation might suggest it is some aspect of myself I wish to destroy. So I contemplate for some time the option of cutting his throat with a carving knife. Stabbing him through the ribs is another possibility I toy with. Both actions are available as plausible narratives, and their being available suffices, it seems, to diffuse the threat of his intimidating presence. Carrying out the actions becomes unnecessary, it is enough to simply imagine them, and the substance of the menace, in fact even the existence of my aggressor, becomes questionable, as though the progress of events has irrevocably altered the nature of their beginnings, and what appeared to be a tale about conflict and violence is now open to promiscuous possibilities. I lash out. The energy and ferocity of my punches are enough to render invisible an enemy with whom I never make contact. The darkness before me is an empty void, my fists meeting nothing but air, the face of the fiend not even glimpsed. Or I rehearse again in my mind a kick to the ribs, to the head, of my floored opponent, admiring the balletic grace of my invincibility as if I were a spectator. I replay these highlights at will, watching in slow motion the jolt of his head as my boot connects with his jaw.

A SECRET

What Ning and Chantal said to each other while they were closeted in Chantal's bedroom remains a mystery. Something vitally important to the unfolding of this story I suspect, though I can't be sure. When they came out of the room they were unusually animated, and straight away their conversation struck me as artificial. It was as though they were playacting, performing a charade for my benefit with the intention of throwing me off the scent. Are they aware of my eavesdropping? I have recorded every word of their conversations since, but they give no clue as to what passed between them that afternoon. They avoid any discussion of matters of importance, offering nothing of psychological interest. It's as though they have entered into a pact to keep me in ignorance of their secrets, speaking only of the most trivial matters when in my presence, subjects too dull to be even worth repeating. Are they deliberately thwarting my attempts to bring this narrative to a satisfactory conclusion?

THE BAOBAB TREE

The only existing image of Nigerian artist Rachel Adeboye's painting *The Baobab Tree* is the original work on canvas. Anyone who wants to see it has to make the trip to a private gallery in upstate New York where the picture resides. Reproduction of the image has been expressly forbidden by the artist, and visitors to the gallery are not permitted to take cameras or phones into the room where the painting hangs. The work is of such complexity, covering so many narrative elements, that it's virtually impossible to describe. Despite these obstacles thousands come every year to see the painting, attracted it seems by its very unknownness. 'There's an aura, a sense of mystery about it,' says Lauren Bergoltz, the curator of the gallery. 'At one time the only way to view a famous picture was to go see it physically. Now images are ubiquitous, they no longer have any authority. Adeboye's picture recaptures that sense of uniqueness we all crave.'

ꙅRUGA

The chat bot seemed to work by drawing me into conversation with questions like 'so what's new?' and 'tell me something interesting', and then building a memory of my replies so that over time it could anticipate my interests and prejudices, the questions becoming modified to include more personal references, phrases such as 'you're right there' and 'exactly my view' punctuating the conversation. At times Druga, that was her name, even indulged in a little speculation herself. At first this annoyed me and I began expressing opinions opposite to those I had previously given, even contradicting myself within the same few sentences. Rather than simply mimic my erratic flights of whimsy, Druga started to challenge me with statements like: 'That isn't what you said a few moments ago.' She seemed programmed to move to a more complex level of conversation depending on the behaviour of her interlocutor, the way certain tests get harder if you answer the questions easily and quickly. I tried reading passages of Kant to her, asking her option and to my surprise found her answers perceptive and thought provoking.

The Wedding

Dan and Julia had decided to get married in a large bouncy castle. They thought it would be fun to have the family members wobbling about while a humanist celebrant conducted the ceremony. Guests would be asked to wear appropriate costumes, like characters out of a fairy tale. Julia thought Dan had said 'humourist' celebrant when he first suggested the idea, and she'd been a little upset that he wasn't taking this seriously enough. But the confusion was soon cleared up, and they started making an invitation list. Thirty-two people came, including half a dozen children under the age of ten. One of the highlights was Julia's mother falling over in the middle of the exchange of vows. Dan laughed at this scene a great deal whenever they watched the video.

⊖BJECT NO. 79

Along the Suffolk coast in late 1972, there were a number of sightings of strange pyramidal objects which when handled 'vanished into the air.' One of the more detailed accounts was given by a retired archaeologist, Bryan Maple, who was walking alone along the shingle beach north of Dunwich when he saw something yellow half-buried in the flotsam of dried kelp, timber and old rope. It was about 50 mm tall, with four triangular sides, perfectly symmetrical. Maple bent to pick it up but found the object impossible to lift, its weight astonishing. He knelt, and using both hands was able after much effort to raise it. He examined the exterior for marks but found none. Each side was completely smooth, a uniform matt yellow showing no sign of wear. As he turned the object he felt it becoming lighter, its density suddenly reducing. This change became increasingly rapid and before he realised what was happening the unusual object rose into the air and was carried away in the wind, spiralling up into the sky where he eventually lost sight of it.

⊄IRE

The alarm has been sounding for some time and everyone except Neil has left the office. 'Would you please leave now,' Angela says. As the floor fire warden it's her responsibility to get everyone out. 'It'll just be another drill,' Neil says, staring at his screen. 'I'm in the middle of something.' 'I don't care what you're doing,' Angela says. 'Would you please get out of the building. You're putting us both at risk.' She thinks she can smell smoke. What if there really is a fire? 'Someone probably burnt some toast,' Neil says. She goes to the door and pushes it open. There's smoke drifting up the stairs. 'Neil, there's smoke out here. We've got to leave.' 'Yeah sure,' he says, 'Pull the other one.' The smoke is denser on the next floor down, and she can hear the popping sound of burning wood. She takes off her hi-vis fire warden vest and ties it across her mouth and nose then, holding her breath, plunges through the thick smoke down several flights of stairs to the lower floors, collapsing finally into the arms of a fire officer. 'Anyone else up there?' he asks. 'No,' Angela says, choking for breath. 'No, I'm pretty sure everyone got out.'

ᗺLUE BOoK

In the drawer of his hotel room desk C discovered a small book, its blue cloth cover unmarked by any lettering. He flicked through the opening pages, and was astonished to find he was reading an account of his early infancy, some of the detail previously unknown to him. Jumping ahead he discovered material relating to his late twenties. How far did the book go, he wondered. Did it deal only with the past, or continue to narrate the events of his life still to come? He broke into a cold sweat at the thought, yet the possibility that the simple act of turning the pages might reveal the manner of his own end had a vertiginous attraction. As he sat there wondering what to do he heard a knock at the door. A young woman in a short skirt and halter-top was standing there. 'Would you be interested in having sex by any chance?' she said. 'I was supposed to be seeing someone in room 182, but there's no one there.' 'Actually, I'm busy with something,' C said distractedly. 'But…you might be able to help. I've been reading a book, the biography of someone I'm interested in. I don't want to know the details of how it ends, but I do want to know if it describes his death. Can I show it to you?' The woman agreed and C ushered her into his room. 'But this is so weird,' she said, reading the final page. 'What is this book? It ends with a young woman knocking at a man's hotel room door, and offering him sex.'

⑬ELIVERED BY HAND

Dear Madam

I had the misfortune to be in the audience on Friday night for the performance of 'A Gothic Parade' – what a dull and ridiculous entertainment you make of my life! I'm portrayed as a sort of moody oddball, a man whose music resembled Debussy's (farcical) but not as good. A dyspeptic, cantankerous eccentric, unable to reconcile himself to failure. Mon Dieu!

The pianist's tempos were much too fast – my *Gymnopedies* transformed into jaunty musical baubles, my *Vexations* (which inspired Cage and Feldman) presented as the outpourings of a wounded heart – absurd!

Can I suggest that next year you engage a pianist who understands my music, and perhaps have someone read from my actual writings (without any half-witted editorial interference), and give your audience a chance to hear my work?

At the end of the performance on Friday, I noticed that a few people in the audience declined to applaud. I salute them heartily! Bravo! It's a pity a few of them didn't have the courage to get up and walk out. I would have done were I not dead and no longer able to defend myself.

With irritation, yours
Erik Satie

⟨ANDROIDS

From the window of the first-floor lounge Lawrence gazes down
on to the garden with its carefully trimmed lawns. 'Having a good
time?' asks the duty supervisor. She's around 30, her face set in
a fixed smile. 'We like our guests to enjoy themselves.' Lawrence
doesn't recall seeing her before, and guesses she must be new. She's
dressed in dark blue Lycra and wearing trainers. 'I'm alright,'
Lawrence says. 'No need to worry.' The woman's face assumes a
look of exaggerated concern as she continues to gaze at him. 'Only
alright?' she says. 'That's not very good is it? Let's see what we can
do to help.' She snaps her fingers and two figures step in from
the next room. They look identical; each dressed in shorts and
Hawaiian shirts, their eyes hidden behind tinted shades. Lawrence
hasn't seen these two before either, and suspects they are androids.
'Our friend here is only feeling "alright",' the woman says. 'We
like to do better than that here don't we?' The androids make a
chuckling sound and take a step forward. 'I'm leaving you in their
capable hands.'

TOPIARY

'Oh yes we've gone completely plastic. The plants they have these days, *so* realistic, you simply can't tell the difference unless you get up really close. No weeding. Chemical sprays take care of that. Flowers in bloom all year round. I don't think we'd ever go back to natural gardening. Even the lawn's artificial, though you'd never guess would you, looking at it from here? No need to mow, and we save a fortune not having to water. Of course it was quite expensive. We went for the *very* best quality we could find. But this is meant to last twenty years. More wine anyone? Without all the hassle you've got time to enjoy life. Show them the topiary, Barry…'

℞ETROSPECTIVE

1. Music of the spheres (1993–94)

A complex array of percussion instruments fills one half of the room: gongs, bells, drums, cymbals, a xylophone, bottles filled with varying levels of coloured liquids, old cans, even a plastic bucket. Drum sticks, spatulas, and brushes attached to levers are connected by a complicated web of strings and pulleys, so that the action of one lever triggers action in another. The machine responds to the movement of people in the room through pressure sensors in the floor. But these effects are delayed, so that the audience don't perceive a relationship between their movements and the sounds produced. The levers are also activated by the sound made by the instruments, through a feedback loop, so that once started the ensemble never stops. The music has no observable pattern. It is purely the product of chance.

2. The ancestors are angry (1998)

The gallery space is dark and a grainy video is showing on the smooth, white wall at the far end. We see puppets with grotesque faces, or perhaps wearing masks. An observer will be reminded of Javanese puppets, or kabuki theatre, the faces of figures in the paintings of Hieronymus Bosch, or of Hallowe'en masks. The puppets are dressed in extravagant costumes, displaying eclectic historical and cultural influences. Skull caps, ruffs, long embroi-dered robes, silk slippers, wide cotton trousers, necklaces of shells and teeth, fur cuffs, and jeweled clasps are visible at various moments. The video is black and white, but occasionally flickers into washed-out colour, the palette dominated by reds and greens.

The background is unfocused, brooding. The figures move jerkily on faintly visible strings, jiggling erratically, sometimes hitting or colliding with each other. The sound track is of a violent storm with heavy rain and thunder.

3. Still life with fruit (2009)

There's a single, round window high up in one of the walls, through which light falls on to a circular table of about the same diameter as the window. A white cloth covers the table, hanging all the way to the floor. On the table is a large glass bowl holding an ostentatious display of exotic fruit. The fruit is rotting, and covered with tiny black flies which rise in a cloud when disturbed. A sickly odour of decay fills the room. Beside the bowl is the skull of a small mammal or bird. Cramped, cursive lines in black ink cover the cranium, the script so small an observer has to lean in close to decipher the text. The smell and the flies deter all but the most inquisitive. A few words only can be made out: 'corruption', 'trickery', 'lies'.

4. I do so *adore* the sea (2014)

A conveyor belt runs across the width of the room at its far end, entering through a hole curtained off by grey cloth strips, and disappearing into a void on the other side. Various items of plastic waste are strewn on the belt. An elderly man in a raincoat is running along the belt towards the grey curtain, matching the speed at which the belt is moving, so that he never makes progress. A woman in a fur coat, heels, and enormous sunglasses enters through a door to the right, followed by a short, officious young man in a white suit and pink tie. He is carrying a folding canvas chair. They stop in front of the audience and the young man starts to unfold the chair, but the woman moves on a few steps, then back, as though trying to decide where to sit. 'I do so *adore* the sea,' she says, heavily stressing the word 'adore'. She peers out at the audience, beams. The man with the chair darts about trying in vain to position it for her. This continues for several minutes. Periodically the old man on the conveyor belt stumbles and falls over, and the belt grinds to a halt. He picks himself up, and the belt starts up again. We hear ten second bursts of Morecambe and Wise singing 'Bring me sunshine' at random intervals, always the same ten seconds. The performers appear oblivious of the music. Eventually the woman leaves the way she came in, followed by the man with the chair, and the room is plunged into darkness.

cAIRPORT

The airport is busy and there's quite a crowd heading down the corridor to Ted's departure gate. As he shuffles along, buffeted by other travellers, a young, smartly-dressed woman with a wheelie-suitcase cuts across in front of him, causing him to trip and fall. 'Ouch,' he says, landing on the suitcase and painfully twisting his left ankle. The woman stares down at him, annoyed. 'I can't believe you did that,' she says. 'Don't you pay attention to the people around you?' Ted is too dazed to respond. 'This is so embarrassing,' she says to the group of passengers starting to form a circle around them. 'You can't even walk through an airport without some idiot colliding with you.' No one makes a move to help Tedl up. His ankle is throbbing and he doesn't think he'll be able to stand, let alone walk. 'Some people have no consideration for others,' the woman says. Several of the bystanders nod and murmur sympathetically. Just then Ted notices his phone starting to vibrate in his coat pocket. It's his daughter calling. 'Oh my God,' the woman says addressing the swelling crowd of onlookers. One or two of them laugh. 'Can you believe this? He's lying on my luggage, I have a plane to catch, and he's about to take a call?'

ℰPISODE 26

'I'm basically a pessimist,' Bill tells Frank. 'A determinist. I believe that everything we do, and think, is essentially programmed in advance. Each of us is acting out a script, expressing beliefs we cannot choose but hold. It's all instinct.' He pauses to take a mouthful of beer. Frank is looking sceptical. 'Of course this has serious implications for morality. If there's no free will, there's no such thing as right or wrong. You can't condemn someone for something they can't help doing, though that wouldn't necessarily stop you locking them up. And there's no such thing as objective truth, which has big implications for science.' 'But if this belief of yours is correct,' Frank interrupts, 'you're also acting out a script, articulating a view which was predetermined, like any other person's view, and which you have no choice but to believe.' 'Yes I've thought of that,' Bill says. 'Am I in effect a machine? Or do I just think I'm a machine because that's the way I've been programmed?'

A CUP OF TEA

While we were having tea at Mrs Tattinger's, a young man I hadn't seen before came into the living room. He was bare-chested, in knee-length shorts, and pulling on a length of rope, as though hauling something in from the garden. Mrs Tattinger seemed not to notice. After a great deal of effort he managed to cross the room, disappearing off to the left, I assume into one of the bedrooms, where he appeared to be securing the rope. He then crossed back and went out through the door he'd entered by, disconnected the rope from its load, and re-crossed the living room, carefully coiling the rope as he went. I wondered if this might be the nephew she had once talked about. I took another sip of tea and asked about her rheumatism. After a few minutes the young man reappeared, entering once again from the same door as before, and the whole procedure was repeated. Still Mrs Tattinger gave no sign of being aware of his presence. It was only during the fourth occurrence, and then without looking up, that she called out to him: 'You ought to stop for a cup of tea.' He seemed not to hear and continued to persevere with his task as though we didn't exist.

H

I hadn't seen H in a long time. She was little changed, and we soon re-established the easy intimacy we had once shared. We were standing in a meadow of tall grass, with no one else in sight. It was high summer, and the warmth of the late afternoon sun made us languorous. H was wearing a loose, sleeveless dress of pale cotton which perfectly became her. She was aroused and slid the dress slowly over her left shoulder, playfully revealing her naked breast. I began to caress her, but as I did so the breast started to take on the shape and features of a child's head, which rapidly matured into those of a fully-grown man. The face seemed vaguely familiar though I couldn't quite place who it was. It was smaller than life size and unmoving, like a waxwork. As I held her breast the flesh turned to stone, and the head fell sideways into the grass where it landed upright, a small plinth sprouting from the neck. H adjusted the dress to cover the place where her breast had been, and bent forward to examine the curious object. It seemed to be suffused by a warm, pink glow, as from a hidden spotlight suspended above our heads.

STRAWBERRIES

The strawberries were the largest Phil had ever seen – some approaching the size of mangoes. They were growing along the bank to the side of the path, perhaps a hundred plants, like mutant aliens from a 1950s B movie. Many of the fruits had deformities, small extra protuberances, and in a few cases forked bodies. He had been thinking of picking some and taking them back to work to share with his colleagues, but now he wasn't so sure. Were they safe to eat? There was no sign advising against it. He bent over to smell the strange fruit but they seemed to be odourless. As he stood there hesitating he became aware of a strong scent of cheap perfume, and turned to find a small woman in a pale raincoat, sky-blue running shoes, and a green visor. She seemed to be watching him. 'Know anything about these strawberries?' Phil asked. 'The sins of the fathers,' the woman said. 'They'll set your teeth on edge.'

☉BJECT NO. 68

25 May 1972: It's as though the community has been struck by pestilence – though we can find no physical cause for their 'sickness'. Only the initiated, the shamans who are dead, had ever seen the sacred object, and its name in the local language, from which the tribe itself derives its identity, is 'that which is nameless and cannot be described.' The timber and grass structure which housed the sacred mysteries contains a few clay pots, some dried plant materials, and stones marked with signs. None of us knows if any of these are the nameless object vital to the tribe's communication with the spirit world. Without language with which to describe it the survivors have no way of knowing whether the spirits have abandoned them or are simply hiding.

OVER-RATED

On Thursday night my wife and I went to the annual concert organised by our local Chamber Music Society, though neither of us could remember why we had bought tickets. The programme was advertised as Mozart followed by Brahms, but just before the start of this 'musical feast' a chap in red trousers got up and announced that the musicians had decided to play the two works in reverse order, Brahms first, followed by Mozart. You can imagine the stir this caused. Well into the first movement of the Brahms much of the audience still looked perplexed, and some never seemed to recover at all from the confusion. The musicians, able professionals though they were, played with a studied lack of emotion, very little attack and a complete absence of dynamics, no doubt in deference to the audience, many of whom like to sleep through the concert, and rouse themselves only when an opportunity to clap presents itself. So effective were the players in their approach to the music that I was soon left wondering why we had ever liked Brahms, and by the end of the fourth movement I was convinced I had badly over-rated him.

THE CHARACTER

Something strange was happening. There was a pattern, the sequence of past events seeming in retrospect to have been pre-determined, each unpredictable step planned out for me. Every move had led inevitably to the next, though at the time they had appeared to be only a series of chance encounters. When I tried to reason this through, to evaluate my options and determine the best course open to me, I found I was doing exactly what I had resolved not to do. Though seeming to choose freely, I had apparently been hoodwinked by my own hidden impulses, though to what end I could not determine. Events, I found, might at any moment take an arbitrary turn, evolving in new and unexpected ways. There was no logic or coherence to this, other than its foreseeable inco-herence. I was frequently surprised, thrown off course, discovering myself not to be the person I had imagined, but someone capable of acts which I had believed alien to my principles, actions which left me wondering if I had any integrity at all. Was I merely the plaything of forces I could not control and only glimpsed in-directly, a trace refracted in my own response, viewed after the fact like a shadow passing, a change in the intensity of the light so quick and subtle I could not be sure I hadn't simply blinked? I felt as though I were being worked by invisible strings, dancing like a puppet to another's will, and yet I could not just give myself over to that superior power. When I stopped striving I was quickly over-whelmed by a sense of lassitude. Nothing buoyed me up, nothing took control of me when I ceased to struggle. I felt the existence of my restraints only when I tried to move, and the more I fought the more aware I was of my dependency. It was precisely when I was most convinced that I was acting rationally, according to my own designs, weighing the pros and cons of an action carefully, exerting all my mental and moral strength, that I became conscious of the fallacy of my independence and knew, from the evidence of my erratic conduct, that I was in fact the product of someone else's imagination.

What we did

Howard had heard his wife speak of their various trips so many times over the years he could almost predict the exact phrases she would use. Each time they met new people at a party, or on holiday, she'd offer up these mementos. But lately he'd noticed that the stories had been changing. She had started adding fresh material, details he didn't recall. There was the trip to Thailand for example, where she claimed they had visited a temple in Bangkok decorated with broken crockery. He had no memory of this. She described a church in Mexico where the corpse of a young girl, preserved by the dry atmosphere, was on display in the crypt. Again he had no recollection of it. Was he losing his memory? Was she losing hers? He was confused, and didn't know how to talk to her about it. Over the next few months the stories became increasingly elaborate. He began to dread going to social gatherings, wondering what outlandish claim his wife would invent. After she told the story about killing, with her sandal, a three foot long mamba discovered in their tent during a safari in Zambia, he decided to confront her. 'Do you think anyone really cares where we went or what we did?' she said. 'I'm so bored with those rituals we engage in, that seeking of common ground. Are other people telling the truth?'

WILDLIFE HOT SPOT

Every spring Hannah liked to visit the stream where the chub spawned. It was a shallow and stony channel, running behind the backs of houses, with a short stretch visible from the road. She had once lived in a house backing onto the stream, and the annual spawning of the fish had been a well-kept local secret. In the spring sunshine, the females were clearly visible from her garden, suspended above the gravel stream-bed, unloading their eggs. Now Hannah had to take a bus across town to visit the spot. This year, as she turned into the normally quiet street, she was surprised to see a party of school children lined up along the railings. They were dressed as fish. A large information board had been erected, with pictures showing the life cycle of the chub. It appeared the place had been designated a 'wildlife hot spot'. Some of the children were scooping dirt from the gutter and throwing it at the fish, while their teachers looked on. One little girl, Hannah noticed, was holding a crushed beer can which she seemed about to toss into the stream. She was dressed as an angel-fish, in bright orange, ribbons trailing from her fins.

CRUSOE'S PENGUINS

In his account of the years he spent as a castaway on a tropical island, Robinson Crusoe claims that he sighted penguins.* We know the approximate location of Crusoe's island was in the Atlantic ocean, off the coast of northern Brazil. Penguins are common on the western coast of South America, and are found in the Galapagos islands, but their normal habitat does not include the part of the world where Crusoe was shipwrecked. It seems improbable that he would have seen penguins, and scholars have long wrestled with how best to explain the anomaly.

The American academic Wendell G. Beresford appeared to have solved the mystery in 1903 when he put forward the theory that Crusoe had simply made a 'slip of the pen' in a moment of distraction, having no doubt intended to write 'pelican'. Beresford provided persuasive orthographic evidence from a fragment of the original manuscript to support this claim, and for many years this was accepted as the obvious explanation. But the 'evidence' later turned out to have been fabricated.

A rival theory advanced by the British scholar, Richard Bellows, in a study published in 1920, hypothesised that unusual climactic conditions during the year in question had caused a number of penguins to migrate to Crusoe's island. But this theory has now been discredited, following advances in the natural sciences.

Perhaps the most intriguing theory is that put forward by the Mexican meteorologist Claudia Nubes in an article first published in 1989. Nubes suggests that Crusoe may have been the victim of an optical illusion. In certain, very unusual, atmospheric conditions, a low lying band of heated air can act as a kind of magnifying glass. In Crusoe's case, Nubes suggests, a much smaller species of seabird was temporarily enlarged to his view as a result of such conditions, and was confused in Crusoe's mind with the penguin. Nubes' theory assumes that penguins were not among the birds Crusoe managed to kill and eat, which the ambiguity of the relevant passage would allow for. The fact that Crusoe nowhere else mentions penguins also provides some support for this idea.

*'Here was also an infinite number of fowls of many kinds, some which I had seen, and some which I had not seen before, and many of them very good meat, but such as I knew not the names of, except those called penguins.' Daniel Defoe, *Robinson Crusoe*, Oxford World's Classics edition, p.94.

ALICE

After my wife left me I developed an obsession with visiting antique shops. These were not shops selling pieces of genuine value, which I could not have afforded, but places stuffed with bric-a-brac, the everyday possessions of people who had downsized in their later years, or who had died, rooms filled with the accumulated ephemera of numerous house clearances. I was convinced that there were bargains to be found, and even perhaps some rare object worth a small fortune buried under all that junk, awaiting my discovery. I had no interest in getting rich, only in the hunt, the satisfaction of outwitting an inattentive trader, the fulfilment of some primitive hunter-gatherer instinct perhaps. After a while the piles of old crockery, worthless paintings and china ornaments, the trashy holiday souvenirs, and the shelves of books by long-forgotten authors began to weigh on me and the compulsiveness of my obsession started to fade. I found nothing of any great monetary value, but I did acquire a stuffed badger, in perfect condition though minus her glass case, who has since become my intimate companion. I call her Alice. She is next to me now, peering down at this page as I write.

THE BENCH

The benches along the cliff-top all bear commemorative plaques, brief personal tributes to those who once spent happy hours here gazing out to sea. My parents loved the place, and when my mother passed away it seemed natural for my father to want to remember her in this way. So we applied for a bench, and had a small plate engraved 'In loving memory of Grace Simpson', followed by her dates. My father died a few years later and I had no further reason to visit the town. I was an only child, with no lasting ties to the area, and I hadn't been there for some years. Now that I was staying for a couple of days on business I took the opportunity to seek out the bench dedicated to my mother's memory. I had no idea if the seat would still be there but it was, exactly where I remembered it. A second brass plaque, I noticed, had been added to the right of the original one. It read: 'How I wish I had known you – your loving daughter Margaret.'

⊙BJECT NO. 253

When she returned to her hotel room at the end of the day she found her hosts had left her a small gift of appreciation, a doll with cute features and large eyes, dressed in the national costume. It was strangely ageless in appearance, neither child nor adult, a kind of benign goblin, she thought. A card attached to the doll's left arm read: 'Thank you for speaking at our conference'. It was signed by the conference chairman, and beneath the name of this august person were the words 'squeeze me'. She picked up the doll and pressed its torso. Its eyes lit up, and a voice like that of an automated conference-call service intoned: 'Thank you Professor Schmidt for your paper on Nietzsche and the problem of the self-reflexive self. We appreciate it.'

THE COOKER

During the night my nipples had become unusually swollen, and quite sore, and I decided I should go to the local health centre to seek a medical opinion. The doctor turned out to be an ex-lover who I hadn't seen for some time. She asked me if I was free for dinner, and suggested we continue the consultation at her apartment, to which I readily agreed. The building where she lived was close by. It looked run down, and the rooms she occupied were shabby and untidy. She had a casserole already prepared, she said, and asked me to put it in the oven to warm through while she went to deal with a few things. The cooker was ancient and rusting, the controls so worn by use I struggled to work out how to turn the oven on, but eventually I got it going. Meanwhile my ex-lover, the doctor, was nowhere to be found. I had taken my shirt off earlier, expecting to be examined, and I was starting to feel the cold. The skin of my arms had goose-bumps and my nipples were on fire.

LIBERTY

The idea was to buy a live lobster, and to cook it at home. But when it came to putting it in the pan of boiling water, neither of us could bring ourselves to do it. The creature looked so pathetic and helpless, despondent even, if you can say that of a lobster. Clearly there was nothing to do but set it free. But the sea was sixty miles away, and I wasn't sure if it was even the right sort of sea. Shouldn't there be rocks? And how long does a lobster survive out of water? Melanie called the local vet to see if they had any advice. 'We think it's a female,' I heard her saying. 'We've called her Libby, Libby the Lobster, that's short for liberty.' The woman on the other end of the phone was laughing. I could hear her clearly. She laughed for quite a long time, I would even say hysterically. 'Hey, what's so funny?' Melanie kept asking. Then the woman hung up.

OBJET D´ART

The queue along the river bank was orderly, and moving forward steadily as people at the viewing place dispersed and others came up to take their place. News of the event had been posted on social media and an audience had quickly gathered, like a flash-mob. Passers-by and the occasional bemused tourist were soon drawn in. The audience maintained a respectful silence, as requested by the artist in his post. The sleeping figure in front of them wore shabby clothes, his hair dusty and matted, his head resting on a large canvas holdall. He was of African heritage, and not unlike the homeless people often seen along this stretch of the Seine. He lay curled up in the middle of a semi-circular recess at the river's edge, warmed by the October sun, and he seemed to be sleeping. The crowd watched from the path above. Some wondered if this was the artist himself, others thought it might be an actor. Some believed the artist, who used the name 'Filou', wasn't himself present. The sleeping man lay still, scarcely moving for more than an hour, but eventually he began to stir. He looked up, gazed vacantly at the crowd, then rose and began to gather his possessions.

J'AI REVÉ DE TOI

She is standing next to the window looking out on to a garden, her face caught in profile against the light. There is no doubt that this is A, the curve of the mouth is hers, the forehead, the neck. She must be 19, 20, framed by the window of a room I do not recognise, a room I once knew perhaps but have since forgotten. She is wearing a pale cotton t-shirt and denim shorts. Her feet are bare, her blonde hair cut short, the way I remember it. On the t-shirt can just be made out the words: *j'ai revé de toi*. She is completely still, as though I am looking at a photograph of her. Then she turns towards me. 'Do I know you?' she asks.

ꝢEDUSA

Ichika Yamagata's epic work *Medusa* is surely the first true novel of the internet age, a 'book' which exists only as a virtual entity and can have no analogue equivalent in print. Not only is the text three dimensional, it is also constantly changing as passages decay and others are generated by the underlying algorithms. It was twelve years in the making, and Yamagata worked with some of the most advanced developers in the field of artificial intelligence to realise the project.

Given the nature of the 'book' any attempt to summarise it is impossible. Yamagata says that an important influence on her was the final three novels of the American writer David Markson, collages of quotations and anecdotes whose interconnecting themes form a kind of disjointed monologue. Yamagata took the collage idea from Markson but decided to make it multi-dimensional by inserting links into the text which lead the reader in different directions, rather like an interactive movie in which the viewer is able to control the sequence of events in the story. The countless bifurcations, some of which make sideways connections to other pieces of text, create so many variant readings no one can ever hope to comprehend the whole.

To make the experience even more complex there is no stable version. Links break, words corrupt and disappear, and whole passages fade according to random processes. At the same time the program supporting the work creates new sections by searching the internet for suitable material which can be incorporated into the novel's architecture and linked to existing content. Even the initial text, about the figures in Greek mythology known as the Gorgons, may not be the original starting point. The association between the work's title and the opening quotation could be purely coincidental, the original opening now residing in some remote branch of the structure, no longer recognisable as a beginning.

ᴀCKNOWLEDGEMENTS

I would like to thank the editors of the following magazines and websites where most of these texts have appeared over the last few years: *Brittle Star, Café Irreal, Decals of Desire, Flash, Fortnightly Review, Ink, Sweat & Tears, International Times, Junction Box, Lighthouse, Neon, Stride,* and *Tears in the Fence.*

About the Author

Simon Collings lives in Oxford, UK. He is a Contributing Editor of *The Fortnightly Review*. His website is https://simoncollings.wordpress.com/

Printed in Great Britain
by Amazon

54163276R00061